D0597162

ABOUT THE BOOK

Ben Gizzard would die on the day he saw a white mountain upside down and a black bird talked to him, but not before. An old Indian he cheated out of some furs told him this.

This was good news to a man as mean and crafty as Ben Gizzard. He settled in treeless, birdless Depression Gulch and cheated, robbed, and killed his way to riches. How his life seemed charmed in that place where there were neither mountains nor birds!

But one day a young artist arrived in town with a large black bird riding on his shoulder. Oh, Ben Gizzard!

Our slithering villain comes to his end when he least expects it, and the world is a better place without him, and a better place for the telling of his story, which is both funny and awesome.

Books by Richard Kennedy

THE RISE AND FALL
OF BEN GIZZARD

Weekly Reader Books presents

THE RISE AND FALL OF BEN GIZZARD

By Richard Kennedy

Illustrated by Marcia Sewall

An Atlantic Monthly Press Book
Little, Brown and Company
BOSTON   TORONTO

TEXT COPYRIGHT © 1978 BY RICHARD KENNEDY

ILLUSTRATIONS COPYRIGHT 1978 © BY MARCIA SEWALL

Library of Congress Cataloging in Publication Data

Kennedy, Richard.
   The rise and fall of Ben Gizzard.

   "An Atlantic Monthly Press book."
   SUMMARY: When he least expects it, a cunning
swindler's good fortune runs out.
   [1. Western stories.   2. Humorous series]
I. Sewall, Marcia.   II. Title.
PZ7.K385Ri   [Fic]   78-1816
ISBN 0-316-48903-4

ATLANTIC—LITTLE, BROWN BOOKS

ARE PUBLISHED BY

LITTLE, BROWN AND COMPANY

IN ASSOCIATION WITH

THE ATLANTIC MONTHLY PRESS

*Published simultaneously in Canada
by Little, Brown & Company (Canada) Limited*

PRINTED IN THE UNITED STATES OF AMERICA

For

Daphne
Alexey
Juris
Benjamin

BEN GIZZARD's mule coughed up blood in the morning, and Ben knew it was dying, so before sunset he traded the doomed beast to an old Indian for a bundle of furs. Ben squatted near the Indian's fire and told some lies to make the deal, which came natural to him, like being ugly. As he was making set to leave, the old Indian threw out a handful of sticks onto the ground and studied the future of the universe in them. He told Ben how he was going to die.

"A white mountain and a black bird," said the old man.

"What's that?" grunted Ben, hitching up a strap on his pack.

The Indian stared at the pattern of sticks. "The day will come when you will see a white mountain upside down, and just then a black bird will talk to you. On that day you will die."

Ben laughed, tossed the furs over his shoulder, and took to the trail again. Ben had no use for Indian witchcraft or anything else he couldn't lay his hands on. He was a shrewd trader and a mean man, and he figured a fellow could get along just fine in the world if he kept watching things out of the corners of his eyes. Ben's eyes had grown long and narrow over the years. He could stand in one spot and look right around the corner of something good, and right behind it, and see the bad part of it.

When he walked into Depression Gulch a few days later, he stuck up a tent and began looking around for someone to take advantage of. The sides of the gulch came right down to the main street, which was nothing but tents and a few shacks. Everyone was mining silver. The gulch was so narrow and high that the sun didn't come up till ten in the morning, and it set at two in the afternoon, but when it gave that narrow treeless alley some light, the outcroppings of silver on the sides of the gulch shone like fillings in a dark mouth, and the mines went in like cavities. Ben examined some of the digs and traded some furs for a claim a widow had, then swindled her out of her dead husband's tools and got to work.

There was silver yet in the diggings, and Ben swung his pick in the small mine. He worked for a week before the mine caved in on him. But by great luck a beam fell and stuck right above him,

protecting him from the smothering fall of dirt and rocks. He waited in his small pocket of air and listened to the rescuers digging toward him. Ben wondered at his good luck to be alive. He remembered what the old Indian had said, that he would not die until the day he saw a white mountain upside down, and a black bird talked to him. You could see no mountain from the bottom of Depression Gulch, and no birds lived in the place. Ben wondered about this, lying there in the dark with his eyes open.

Ben kept working at his mine. It was just a week later when he had another close call. Ben and some other men were hanging around a dynamite shack when it blew up. Three men were killed in the explosion, but Ben wasn't even hurt. Even as he was flying through the air toward the bush that would gently catch him, Ben remembered what the old Indian had said about the white mountain and the black bird. He landed without a scratch.

That night Ben lay in his blankets and wondered some more. Twice he should have been killed, but he got out of it. What if the fortune the old Indian told was true? If it was, treeless, birdless Depression Gulch might be a very good place for a man like Ben Gizzard. If the old Indian *had* seen into the future and seen truly, then Ben could be as reckless as he wanted. He could cheat and swindle without a worry of being hanged or shot for it, and take any sort of chance to get above everybody else. The day would not come to Depression Gulch when he would die for his wickedness. Ben began waiting for one more proof of it.

The proof soon came. Two days later Ben was in the silver assayer's office when eight robbers rode into Depression Gulch and began shooting their way through town. They ripped up tents, shot out windows, set fires, loaded up with silver and killed anyone in their way. When they reached the assay office, Ben stepped out with two borrowed six-guns and faced them. Standing very still and quiet, with the robbers' bullets flying all around him, Ben took slow and careful aim and shot every single robber off his horse, one by one. Ben stood there in perfect health and watched them getting dragged off to the undertakers by their boot heels. He looked up and around the town. Not a mountain in sight, not a bird.

That day, Ben Gizzard was made sheriff, and

thereafter Depression Gulch was safe from all robbers except Ben Gizzard himself. He began bossing the town and making up laws. He got an office and started getting rich by making up laws and fining the people for breaking them. He set up a bank and made himself president of it. He built a courthouse and made himself judge, and got richer by stealing property and goods legally in trials. The town grew, and Ben held an election for mayor. He won the job because no one dared to run against him. When Ben had trouble with anybody, he found a weak excuse and simply shot him down. He never got hurt himself. There were no birds in Depression Gulch, and no mountains to be seen. Naturally, the townsfolk were afraid of a man so powerful who seemed to be charmed against any harm.

Now it was Mayor Ben Gizzard. Ben dressed himself in fancy hand-tooled boots, a beaver hat, fine suits and linen shirts with ruffles at the cuffs.

He wore a diamond stickpin and tucked a gold watch in his vest pocket. He carried a silver-knobbed ebony walking stick with which he pushed open doors, rapped heads, and walloped dogs who came sniffing at him.

Ben gave his sheriff's badge to a scarred-up villain who only needed a little violence now and then to keep him relieved and happy. Together, they walked around town causing mischief and misery. Ben would hitch up his pants in satisfaction after a good swindle and say to his sheriff, "I guarantee you I ain't wearing silk shorts because I'm stupid." He used to say that quite often. He was proud of his silk shorts. They reminded him how smart he was. Even the ladies in town wore cotton. That was one of the laws.

There was also a law which the townsfolk considered stranger than the rest. It was this: no books with pictures in them were allowed in town. That was an easy law to keep, so Ben never collected any money on it. That's why the towns-folk thought it strange. But Ben had a good reason for it. He now fully believed what the old Indian had said to him, and he was making certain that there should not even be a *picture* of a white mountain in town. For if such a picture were in a book, then there would always be the chance that Ben might see that book open and upside down at that page. There were no white mountains to be seen, and no birds at all in Depression Gulch. And so what other men dared not do for fear of dying, Ben Gizzard would dare. Ben was perfectly safe to do as he pleased any day, since he would not die on that day, and he could not see forward to the day that he would. The town grew, and Ben became rich. He slid around town like a salamander in his silk shorts, and the cheated townsfolk looked on him with envy, hatred, and fear. Thus was the rise of Ben Gizzard.

One day when the sun was between the cliffs of Depression Gulch, Mayor Ben Gizzard looked out his office window and saw a young man walking into town. He had a pack on his back with a shovel sticking out of it. Ben's heart jumped when he saw him, for perched on the shoulder of the young man was a large black bird. He called out the door to the sheriff, and the two men strolled into the street. They cut into the young man's path and blocked his way.

"Howdy, I'm the mayor," said Ben.

"Hello, my name is Paul," said the young man. The black bird turned his head slowly and looked at Ben with its ancient reptilian eyes, then looked away disdainfully.

"You figure on staying long?" asked Ben. The sheriff circled around the young man, looking him up and down. Paul had no gun.

"I thought I might work some tailings for a bit," Paul said.

Ben nodded. After the mines and sluice boxes were worked there were heaps of discarded earth that contained tiny bits of silver. Those heaps were called tailings, and the miners allowed bums and drifters the small silver they held if anyone wanted to take the trouble to sift it out. It didn't amount to much. Ben looked at the black bird again. He put a fist up and shoved at it. The bird fluttered a wing out to keep its balance, but didn't even look at Ben. Paul frowned, but said nothing.

"Okay," said Ben. "Just watch yourself." He and the sheriff walked back inside.

Ben sat alone at his desk, watching the young man go up the street. He would have found some excuse to shoot him, but the young man appeared so mild and harmless it would have been difficult to give even a poor reason for it. "Well," he mused, rubbing his chin, "a dumb black bird is all, and no mountains around here. I can chase him out anytime." And he tried to forget about it.

17

Paul found an old abandoned shack and set it up for his home. Then he got to working on the tailings. His black bird sat on his shoulder as he worked. He didn't work much, only a couple of hours a day, just enough to buy his food, and he seemed innocent of any intent except to lead a peaceful life. But Ben Gizzard kept an eye on him and the black bird.

Paul built a small porch on his shack, and got himself a stove. Blue smoke wove up out of the dark gulch above his place. High up where the smoke flattened out in the wind that swept across Depression Gulch, his black bird flew in wide, soft circles. Each day Ben Gizzard sent the sheriff around to the shack when Paul was in the tailings, and he got his reports.

"What's he up to?" Ben asked.

"Nothing. Just living quiet, far as I can see."

"Okay," said Ben. "Why don't you stick your feet up on the desk and relax." He poured the sheriff and himself a drink and tried not to worry about it.

But one day the report was different.

"What's he up to?" Ben asked.

"Painting a picture in there," the sheriff said, sticking his feet up on Ben's desk.

"Yeah? What kind of picture?"

"Mountain," said the sheriff.

20

Ben jumped to his feet. "Snow-covered mountain?"

"Yeah, so it is."

Ben took a swing at the sheriff's boots. "Get your stinking feet off my desk!" he yelled. The man stumbled to the door.

"Sorry, Mr. Gizzard! Sorry!" said the sheriff, all confusion, looking around the door jamb. Ben was standing with his fists on his desk, grinding his teeth. The sheriff hoped to please him with something else he had found out. "Something else you ought to know, mayor," he said.

"What's that?" snarled Ben.

"He ordered some silk at the Wells Fargo station."

Ben slung a bottle at the man, who jerked his head away just in time. Mayor Ben Gizzard sat down at his desk and bit his fingernails for a while, then stuck his hat on and headed up toward Paul's shack. The door was open. Paul heard Ben come up on the porch.

"Come on in," the young man called out cheerily. Ben ducked his head through the door and went inside. Paul had an easel set up in the center of the room. The black bird was perched on top of it. On the easel was a scrap of old tent canvas nailed to a board, and on it was a painted picture of a perfect cone-shaped white mountain. Ben shot a glance at the bird, which returned the look scornfully and looked out the window.

"Hello, Mayor."

"What's that you're painting?"

"Mountain," said Paul. "Of course it ain't much on this old scrap of canvas, but I ordered some silk to paint it on."

"There ain't no mountain around here," said Ben. "How come a mountain?"

"I dream about it," said Paul, touching his brush gently to the canvas. "I close my eyes to

23

remember it. It's beautiful, just so perfect and smooth and lovely. Of course this canvas is worn and rough, but when I get some silk you'll see how it really should look."

"There ain't going to be no silk," said Ben. "And there's a law in this town that people can't paint dreams. It's a hanging law. Now you understand that?"

"Hanging?" said Paul, looking at the mayor. "You hang people for painting things they see in dreams? I never heard of such a law. And I can't have any silk to paint on? Is that a law, too?"

"That's right," said Ben, taking a slithering hitch on his trousers. "Since you didn't know the law, I won't hang you, but I'm taking that painting for evidence in case you break the law again."

Paul began to argue. Ben shoved him aside and walked over to the easel. He grabbed the painting. But he grabbed too quick and fumbled. The painting fell. It turned in the air as it fell toward

the floor. In that astounding second Ben Gizzard
could see that it was going to land upside down
to him, and out of the wide and watching corner
of his eye he saw that the black bird had jerked
its head toward him and opened its beak as if to
speak. Terror drove through Ben like a spike.

Before the painting hit the floor, Ben clamped his eyes shut and slapped his hands over his ears and blundered out the small door and fell down the porch steps. He ran all the way back to his office and sat sweating at his desk, shaking all over, for he was certain that he had barely escaped his death for seeing a white mountain upside down and hearing a black bird talk to him.

After he had recovered he sent the sheriff up to get the painting. He ordered the man to take it by force, then burn it. The sheriff was back in the mayor's office in a half hour.

"Did you do it?" Ben asked.

"Yup," said the sheriff.

"Put your feet up on the desk and relax," said Ben.

"Sure," said the man. He looked curiously at the mayor and said, "I suppose you got a reason for me doing that?"

Ben hitched his trousers. "I guarantee you I ain't wearing silk shorts because I'm stupid," he said. Yet that night Ben slept poorly, and in the morning he was worried. He sent the sheriff up to Paul's shack for a report.

Ten minutes later, the sheriff returned. "Just painting," he said, tossing his feet up on the mayor's desk.

"What's he painting?" Ben asked.

"Another white mountain, that's all," said the sheriff.

"Get your stinking feet off my desk!" the mayor yelled. The sheriff started for the door, but Ben called him back to sit down. He reached for the bottle and poured each of them a drink, then said, "You know anything about birds?"

"Little."

"Can a black bird talk?"

"Some say so. Raven can anyway. Ravens are holy Indian birds. Indians say they talk all the time."

"That black bird that Paul's got up there — is that a raven?"

"Yup," said the sheriff.

Ben took another drink. "When does Paul come back to his shack?"

"'Bout an hour," said the sheriff. Ben nodded. "Stick your feet up and relax. Here, have another drink." The sheriff was pleased to do both.

He tilted his hat back and smacked his lips at the whiskey.

"When he comes back to the shack," Ben said, "kill him! Kill the bird, too."

The sheriff went back up to the shack when Paul returned. He pretended to visit and admire the painting. When he left he closed the door and put a wedge on it from the outside to trap Paul inside. Then he set the place on fire. But it was a bad job. Paul had a bucket of water handy. He put out the fire and climbed out the window with his bird.

The sheriff came back to the mayor's office and told what had happened. Ben cussed him and decided he'd have to help out with the job himself.

Early the next morning Ben took the sheriff off with him to Paul's shack while Paul was working at the tailings. Directly above the shack was an overhanging cliff with a great boulder balanced on it. Ben told the sheriff to climb up there and drop a string down with a rock on the end of it. The rock dangled directly above the porch, just outside the charred front door. Ben got his man with him again and gave orders.

"You stay up there with the boulder. I'll come around after Paul gets back from the tailings and get him to come out the door. Then I'll look up and nod at you, and you shove the boulder over the cliff. Got that?"

The sheriff nodded. "That's mighty smart, Mr. Gizzard."

"I guarantee you I ain't wearing silk shorts because I'm stupid. Now get up there!"

An hour later, Paul was in his shack painting when Mayor Ben Gizzard came around. Ben stood on the porch steps and greeted Paul in a friendly way, but Paul looked at him suspiciously. Ben squinted through the door. He could see a painting of a snow-covered mountain on the easel. The black bird was perched in its usual place on top of the easel. It glanced at Ben with a cold and weary eye, then looked out the open window.

"Say, painting another mountain, are you?" said Ben, for he had to seem friendly to lure Paul outside onto the porch where the boulder would fall.

"You can't hang me for painting this one, Mr. Gizzard. This one's not a dream mountain. This one's real." Paul spoke a word to the black bird. It jumped from the easel and flew out the window. Up it circled, up and up until it rode

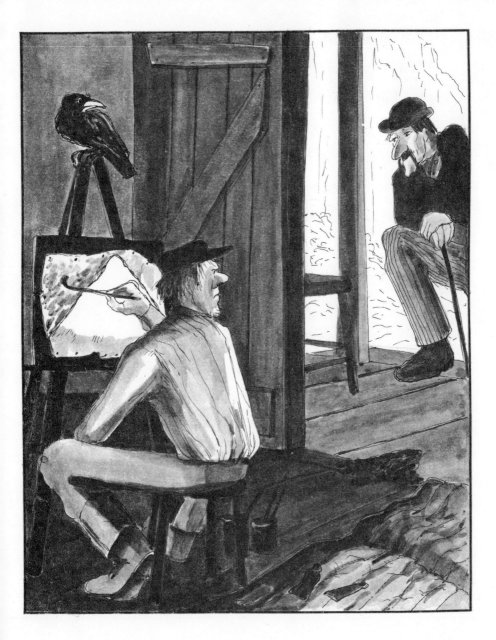

high above Depression Gulch in the free wind. "Way up there my bird sees a real mountain," said Paul, "and he tells me about it, and this is a picture of that mountain."

Ben laughed. "That a fact? Talking bird, eh?" His voice was nervous.

"Yes, sir," said Paul, and he touched at the canvas with his brush.

"Well, Paul, that's great. I wouldn't want to stop you from painting that mountain. I been thinking it over and conclude we need a painter in town. Yes, I been thinking about just that. So you just step out the door here and I'll swear you in and make it all official."

Paul stopped painting and turned to the mayor. "I don't believe you, Mr. Gizzard. You tried to stop me painting once before and I think you tried to burn me out of here. I don't believe you like me at all. You shoved my bird first time we met and you won't let me have any silk or paint

34

my dreams, and I think you're trying to hurt me."

"Oh, Paul, that's not so!" said Ben. "Just step out here and we'll talk this over."

"Didn't the sheriff try to burn down my place?"

"Oh, no, Paul, no! Listen, we *need* a painter. I'll get you a gold medal to wear that says 'Town Painter' on it."

"And I could paint my dreams?" Paul asked. He was beginning to believe Ben, who, like a snake, had a way of getting up close and confidential before he struck.

"Dreams, memories, visions, miracles . . . anything," said Ben. "Take my word for it."

Paul laid his brush down and took a step toward the door. "And you'll let me have some silk to paint on?"

"Of course, Paul. Silk or satin or velvet or anything."

Paul hesitated. "I still don't know if I believe you, Mr. Gizzard."

"Listen, Paul," said Ben. "Look here." He stooped and slid off one fancy boot, then the other, and unbuckled the great silver buckle on his trousers. "Paul, you can have all the silk you want, and I'll give you some to start on right now. I just want to show you my heart's in the right place." And he dropped his trousers.

Ben was wearing light blue silk shorts with just the faintest yellow line in them and a delicate pattern of pale pink flowers. Paul stepped to the very entrance of the door to look at this wonder of the undergarment trade. He was one step away from the place where the boulder would come crashing down.

"Just take one more step out here, Paul," said Ben, "and I'll strip these silk shorts off and hand them right to you." He stepped out of his trousers and kicked them aside. Mayor Ben Gizzard stood there in his bare legs, smiling, and innocent Paul, finally fooled, took the step out the door.

Ben Gizzard looked up. He nodded, and the boulder rolled off the cliff and fell.

Ben thought he had it perfectly calculated. He stood still, smiling friendly at Paul to hold him in place, thumbs hooked in the top of his shorts as if he was ready to peel them off. The boulder fell, and Ben had calculated wrong. The great rock hit neither of them, but fell just three feet from Ben, landing on the opposite end of the step he was standing on. Ben was shot up into the air like a missile out of a catapult. The air rushed past him and the shack grew small below him. Ben was shaken and surprised, but he knew he would land safely, probably in a water trough or a basket of washing, so he wasn't too worried.

At the very top of the arc, far above Depression Gulch, Ben hung motionless in the air for a deep and silent moment, turning slowly before he started down again. And in that moment, feet pointed into the sky, he saw in the distance, up-

side down, an enormous snow-covered mountain. Then just for a wink the mountain was blocked out by the dark shape of Paul's black bird, which flew past with its head turned toward Ben. And considering that Ben had been so mean to Paul, the bird gave him a nice compliment.

"Howdy there, Mayor!" it said. "Them's mighty smart-looking shorts you got on."

Then Ben Gizzard began falling.

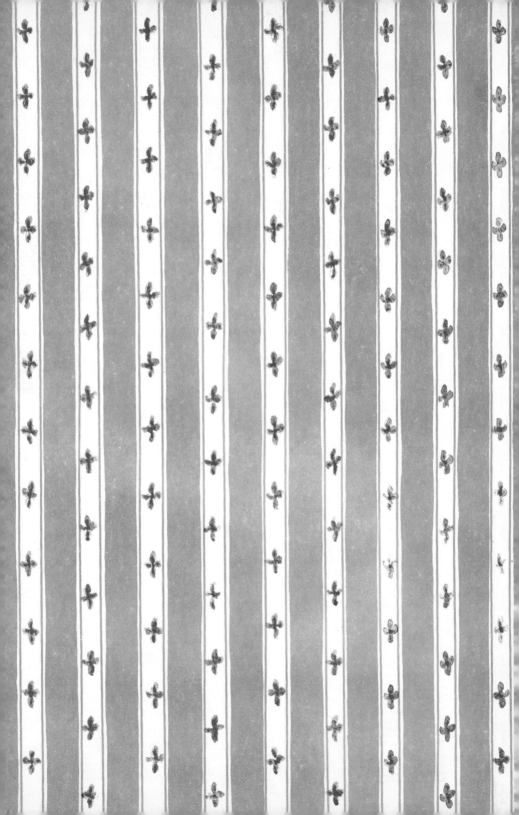